Concerning the Jews

Mark Twain

D1416555

Contents

Some months ago I published a magazine article descriptive of a remarkable scene in the Imperial Parliament in Vienna. Since then I have received from Jews in America several letters of inquiry. They were difficult letters to answer, for they were not very definite. But at last I have received a definite one. It is from a lawyer, and he really asks the questions which the other writers probably believed they were asking. By help of this text I will do the best I can to publicly answer this correspondent, and also the others—at the same time apologizing for having failed to reply privately. The lawyer's letter reads as follows:

I have read 'Stirring Times in Austria.' One point in particular is of vital import to not a few thousand people, including myself, being a point about which I have often wanted to address a question to some disinterested person. The show of military force in the Austrian Parliament, which precipitated the riots, was not introduced by any Jew. No Jew was a member of that body. No Jewish question was involved in the Ausgleich or in the language proposition. No Jew was insulting anybody. In short, no Jew was doing any mischief toward anybody whatsoever. In fact, the Jews were the only ones of the nineteen different races in Austria which did not have a party — they are absolutely non-participants.

Yet in your article you say that in the rioting which followed, all classes of people were unanimous only on one thing, viz., in being against the Jews. Now will you kindly tell me why, in your judgment, the Jews have thus ever been, and are even now, in these days of supposed intelligence, the butt of baseless, vicious animosities? I dare say that for centuries there has been no more quiet, undisturbing, and well-behaving citizen, as a class, than that same Jew. It seems to me that ignorance and fanaticism cannot alone account for these horrible and unjust persecutions.

"Tell me, therefore, from your vantage-point of cold view, what in your mind is the cause. Can American Jews do anything to correct it either in America or abroad? Will it ever come to an end? Will a Jew be permitted to live honestly, decently, and peaceably like the rest of mankind? What has become of the Golden Rule?" I will begin by saying that if I thought myself prejudiced against the Jew, I should hold it fairest to leave this subject to a person not crippled in that way. But I think I have no such prejudice. A few years ago a Jew observed to me that there was no uncourteous reference to his people in my books, and asked how it happened. It happened because the disposition was lacking. I am quite sure that (bar one) I have no race prejudices, and I think I have no color prejudices nor caste prejudices nor creed prejudices. Indeed, I know it.

I can stand any society. All that I care to know is that a man is a human being — that is enough for me; he can't be any worse. I have no special regard for Satan; but I can at least claim that I have no prejudice against him. It may even be that I lean a little his way, on account of his not having a fair show.

All religions issue bibles against him, and say the most injurious things about him, but we never hear his side. We have none but the evidence for the prosecution, and yet we have rendered the verdict. To my mind, this is irregular. It is un-English; it is un-American; it is French. Without this precedent Dreyfus could not have been condemned.

Of course Satan has some kind of a case, it goes without saying. It may be a poor one, but that is nothing; that can be said about any of us. As soon as I can get at the facts I will undertake his rehabilitation myself, if I can find an unpolitic publisher. It is a thing which we ought to be willing to do for any one who is under a cloud. We may not pay him reverence, for that would be indiscreet, but we can at least respect his talents.

A person who has for untold centuries maintained the imposing position of spiritual head of four-fifths of the human race, and political head of the whole of it, must be granted the possession of executive abilities of the loftiest order. In his large presence the other popes and politicians shrink to midges for the microscope. I would like to see him. I would rather see him and shake him by the tail than any other member of the European Concert.

In the present paper I shall allow myself to use the word Jew as if it stood for both religion and race. It is handy; and, besides, that is what the term means to the general world. In the above letter one notes these points:

1. The Jew is a well-behaved citizen.
2. Can ignorance and fanaticism alone account for his unjust treatment?
3. Can Jews do anything to improve the situation?
4. The Jews have no party; they are non-participants.
5. Will the persecution ever come to an end?
6. What has become of the Golden Rule?

Point No. 1.

We must grant proposition No. 1 for several sufficient reasons. The Jew is not a disturber of the peace of any country. Even his enemies will concede that. He is not a loafer, he is not a sot, he is not noisy, he is not a brawler nor a rioter, he is not quarrelsome. In the statistics of crime his presence is conspicuously rare — in all countries. With murder and other crimes of violence he has but little to do: he is a stranger to the hangman. In the police court's daily long roll of "assaults" and "drunk and disorderlies" his name seldom appears.

That the Jewish home is a home in the truest sense is a fact which no one will dispute. The family is knitted together by the strongest affections; its members show each other every due respect; and reverence for the elders is an inviolate law of the house. The Jew is not a burden on the charities of the state nor of the city; these could cease from their functions without affecting him.

When he is well enough, he works; when he is incapacitated, his own people take care of him. And not in a poor and stingy way, but with a fine and large benevolence. His race is entitled to be called the most benevolent of all the races of men. A Jewish beggar is not impossible, perhaps; such a thing may exist, but there are few men that can say they have seen that spectacle. The Jew has been staged in many uncomplimentary forms, but, so far as I know, no dramatist has done him the injustice to stage him as a beggar. Whenever a Jew has real need to beg, his people save him from the necessity of doing it. The charitable institutions of the Jews are supported by Jewish money, and amply. The Jews make no noise about it; it is done quietly; they do not nag and pester and harass us for contributions; they give us peace, and set us an example — an example which we have not found ourselves able to follow; for by nature we are not free givers, and have to be patiently and persistently hunted down in the interest of the unfortunate.

These facts are all on the credit side of the proposition that the Jew is a good and orderly citizen. Summed up, they certify that he is quiet, peaceable, industrious, unaddicted to high crimes and brutal dispositions; that his family life is commendable; that he is not a burden upon public charities; that he is not a beggar; that in benevolence he is above the reach of competition. These are the very quint-essentials of good citizenship. If you can add that he is as honest as the average of his neighbors — But I think that question is affirmatively answered by the fact that he is a successful business man.

The basis of successful business is honesty; a business cannot thrive where the parties to it cannot trust each other. In the matter of numbers of the Jew counts for little in the overwhelming population of New York; but that his honesty counts for much is guaranteed by the fact that the immense wholesale business houses of Broadway, from the Battery to Union Square, is substantially in his hands. I suppose that the most picturesque example in history of a trader's trust in his fellow-trader was one where it was not Christian trusting Christian, but Christian trusting Jew.

That Hessian Duke who used to sell his subjects to George III. to fight George Washington with got rich at it; and by-and-by, when the wars engendered by the French Revolution made his throne too warm for him, he was obliged to fly the country. He was in a hurry, and had to leave his earnings behind — $9,000,000. He had to risk the money with some one without security. He did not select a Christian, but a Jew — a Jew of only modest means, but of high character; a character so high that it left him lonesome — Rothschild of Frankfort. Thirty years later, when Europe had become quiet and safe again, the Duke came back from overseas, and the Jew returned the loan, with interest added.[1]

The Jew has his other side. He has some discreditable ways, though he has not a monopoly of them, because he cannot get entirely rid of vexatious Christian competition. We have seen that he seldom transgresses the laws against crimes of violence. Indeed, his dealings with courts are almost restricted to matters connected with commerce. He has a reputation for various small forms of cheating, and for practising oppressive usury, and for burning himself out to get the insurance, and for arranging cunning contracts which leave him an exit but lock the other man in, and for smart evasions which find him safe and comfortable just within the strict letter of the law, when court and jury know very well that he has violated the spirit of it.

He is a frequent and faithful and capable officer in the civil service, but he is charged with an unpatriotic disinclination to stand by the flag as a soldier — like the Christian Quaker. Now if you offset these discreditable features by the creditable ones summarized in a preceding paragraph beginning with the words, "These facts are all on the credit side," and strike a balance, what must the verdict be? This, I think: that, the merits and demerits being fairly weighed and measured on both sides, the Christian can claim no superiority over the Jew in the matter of good citizenship. Yet in all countries, from the dawn of history, the Jew has been persistently and implacably hated, and with frequency persecuted.

Point No. 2.

"Can fanaticism alone account for this?"

Years ago I used to think that it was responsible for nearly all of it, but latterly I have come to think that this was an error. Indeed, it is now my conviction that it is responsible for hardly any of it. In this connection I call to mind Genesis, chapter xlvii. We have all thoughtfully — or unthoughtfully — read the pathetic story of the years of plenty and the years of famine in Egypt, and how Joseph, with that opportunity, made a corner in broken hearts, and the crusts of the poor, and human liberty — a corner whereby he took a nation's money all away, to the last penny; took a nation's livestock all away, to the last hoof; took a nation's land away, to the last acre; then took the nation itself, buying it for bread, man by man, woman by woman, child by child, till all were slaves; a corner which took everything, left nothing; a corner so stupendous that, by comparison with it, the most gigantic corners in subsequent history are but baby things, for it dealt in hundreds of millions of bushels, and its profits were reckonable by hundreds of millions of dollars, and it was a disaster so crushing that its effects have not wholly disappeared from Egypt to-day, more than three thousand years after the event.

Is it presumable that the eye of Egypt was upon Joseph the foreign Jew all this time? I think it likely. Was it friendly? We must doubt it. Was Joseph establishing a character for his race which would survive long in Egypt? and in time would his name come to be familiarly used to express that character — like Shylock's? It is hardly to be doubted.

Let us remember that this was centuries before the crucifixion. I wish to come down eighteen hundred years later and refer to a remark made by one of the Latin historians. I read it in a translation many years ago, and it comes back to me now with force. It was alluding to a time when people were still living who could have seen the Savior in the flesh. Christianity was so new that the people of Rome had hardly heard of it, and had but confused notions of what it was.

The substance of the remark was this: Some Christians were persecuted in Rome through error, they being "mistaken for Jews." The meaning seems plain. These pagans had nothing against Christians, but they were quite ready to persecute Jews. For some reason or other they hated a Jew before they even knew what a Christian was. May I not assume, then, that the persecution of Jews is a thing which antedates Christianity and was not born of Christianity? I think so.

What was the origin of the feeling? When I was a boy, in the back settlements of the Mississippi Valley, where a gracious and beautiful Sunday-school simplicity and unpracticality prevailed, the "Yankee" (citizen of the New England States) was hated with a splendid energy. But religion had nothing to do with it. In a trade, the Yankee was held to be about five times the match of the Westerner. His shrewdness, his insight, his judgment, his knowledge, his enterprise, and his formidable cleverness in applying these forces were frankly confessed, and most competently cursed.

In the cotton States, after the war, the simple and ignorant negroes made the crops for the white planter on shares. The Jew came down in force, set up shop on the plantation, supplied all the negro's wants on credit, and at the end of the season was proprietor of the negro's share of the present crop and of part of his share of the next one. Before long, the whites detested the Jew, and it is doubtful if the negro loved him.

The Jew is being legislated out of Russia. The reason is not concealed. The movement was instituted because the Christian peasant and villager stood no chance against his commercial abilities. He was always ready to lend money on a crop, and sell vodka and other necessaries of life on credit while the crop was growing. When settlement day came he owned the crop; and next year or year after he owned the farm, like Joseph.

In the dull and ignorant England of John's time everybody got into debt to the Jew. He gathered all lucrative enterprises into his hands; he was the king of commerce; he was ready to be helpful in all profitable ways; he even financed crusades for the rescue of the Sepulchre. To wipe out his account with the nation and restore business to its natural and incompetent channels he had to be banished from the realm.

For the like reasons Spain had to banish him four hundred years ago, and Austria about a couple of centuries later. In all the ages Christian Europe has been obliged to curtail his activities. If he entered upon a mechanical trade, the Christian had to retire from it. If he set up as a doctor, he was the best one, and he took the business. If he exploited agriculture, the other farmers had to get at something else. Since there was no way to successfully compete with him in any vocation, the law had to step in and save the Christian from the poor-house.

Trade after trade was taken away from the Jew by statute till practically none was left. He was forbidden to engage in agriculture; he was forbidden to practise law; he was forbidden to practise medicine, except among Jews; he was forbidden the handicrafts. Even the seats of learning and the schools of science had to be closed against this tremendous antagonist.

Still, almost bereft of employments, he found ways to make money, even ways to get rich. Also ways to invest his takings well, for usury was not denied him. In the hard conditions suggested, the Jew without brains could not survive, and the Jew with brains had to keep them in good training and well sharpened up, or starve. Ages of restriction to the one tool which the law was not able to take from him — his brain — have made that tool singularly competent; ages of compulsory disuse of his hands have atrophied them, and he never uses them now.

This history has a very, very commercial look, a most sordid and practical commercial look, the business aspect of a Chinese cheap-labor crusade. Religious prejudices may account for one part of it, but not for the other nine. Protestants have persecuted Catholics, but they did not take their livelihoods away from them. The Catholics have persecuted the Protestants with bloody and awful bitterness, but they never closed agriculture and the handicrafts against them. Why was that? That has the candid look of genuine religious persecution, not a trade-union boycott in a religious disguise.

I feel convinced that the Crucifixion has not much to do with the world's attitude towards the Jew; that the reasons for it are older than that event, as suggested by Egypt's experience and by Rome's regret for having persecuted an unknown quantity called a Christian, under the mistaken impression that she was merely persecuting a Jew. Merely a Jew — a skinned eel who was used to it, presumably.

The Jews are harried and obstructed in Austria and Germany, and lately in France; but England and America give them an open field and yet survive. Scotland offers them an unembarrassed field too, but there are not many takers. There are a few Jews in Glasgow, and one in Aberdeen; but that is because they can't earn enough to get away. The Scotch pay themselves that compliment, but it is authentic.

I am persuaded that in Russia, Austria, and Germany nine-tenths of the hostility to the Jew comes from the average Christian's inability to compete successfully with the average Jew in business — in either straight business or the questionable sort. In Berlin, a few years ago, I read a speech which frankly urged the expulsion of the Jews from Germany; and the agitator's reason was as frank as his proposition.

It was this: that eighty-five per cent. of the successful lawyers of Berlin were Jews, and that about the same percentage of the great and lucrative businesses of all sorts in Germany were in the hands of the Jewish race! Isn't it an amazing confession? It was but another way of saying that in a population of 48,000,000, of whom only 500,000 were registered as Jews, eighty-five per cent. of the brains and honesty of the whole was lodged in the Jews.

I must insist upon the honesty — it is an essential of successful business, taken by and large. Of course it does not rule out rascals entirely, even among Christians, but it is a good working rule, nevertheless. The speaker's figures may have been inexact, but the motive of persecution stands out as clear as day. The man claimed that in Berlin the banks, the newspapers, the theatres, the great mercantile, shipping, mining, and manufacturing interests, the big army and city contracts, the tramways, and pretty much all other properties of high value, and also the small businesses, were in the hands of the Jews.

He said the Jew was pushing the Christian to the wall all along the line; that it was all a Christian could do to scrape together a living; and that the Jew must be banished, and soon — there was no other way of saving the Christian.

Here in Vienna, last autumn, an agitator said that all these disastrous details were true of Austria-Hungary also; and in fierce language he demanded the expulsion of the Jews. When politicians come out without a blush and read the baby act in this frank way, unrebuked, it is a very good indication that they have a market back of them, and know where to fish for votes. You note the crucial point of the mentioned agitation; the argument is that the Christian cannot compete with the Jew, and that hence his very bread is in peril. To human beings this is a much more hate-inspiring thing than is any detail connected with religion.

With most people, of a necessity, bread and meat take first rank, religion second. I am convinced that the persecution of the Jew is not due in any large degree to religious prejudice. No, the Jew is a money-getter; and in getting his money he is a very serious obstruction to less capable neighbors who are on the same quest. I think that that is the trouble.

In estimating worldly values the Jew is not shallow, but deep. With precocious wisdom he found out in the morning of time that some men worship rank, some worship heroes, some worship power, some worship God, and that over these ideals they dispute and cannot unite—but that they all worship money; so he made it the end and aim of his life to get it.

He was at it in Egypt thirty-six centuries ago; he was at it in Rome when that Christian got persecuted by mistake for him; he has been at it ever since. The cost to him has been heavy; his success has made the whole human race his enemy—but it has paid, for it has brought him envy, and that is the only thing which men will sell both soul and body to get.

He long ago observed that a millionaire commands respect, a two-millionaire homage, a multi-millionaire the deepest deeps of adoration. We all know that feeling; we have seen it express itself. We have noticed that when the average man mentions the name of a multi-millionaire he does it with that mixture in his voice of awe and reverence and lust which burns in a Frenchman's eye when it falls on another man's centime.

Point No. 4.

"The Jews have no party; they are non-participants."

Perhaps you have let the secret out and given yourself away. It seems hardly a credit to the race that it is able to say that; or to you, sir, that you can say it without remorse; more than you should offer it as a plea against maltreatment, injustice, and oppression. Who gives the Jew the right, who gives any race the right, to sit still, in a free country, and let somebody else look after its safety?

The oppressed Jew was entitled to all pity in the former times under brutal autocracies, for he was weak and friendless, and had no way to help his case. But he has ways now, and he has had them for a century, but I do not see that he has tried to make serious use of them. When the Revolution set him free in France it was an act of grace — the grace of other people; he does not appear in it as a helper. I do not know that he helped when England set him free. Among the Twelve Sane Men of France who have stepped forward with great Zola at their head to fight (and win, I hope and believe[2]) the battle for the most infamously misused Jew of modern times, do you find a great or rich or illustrious Jew helping?

In the United States he was created free in the beginning — he did not need to help, of course. In Austria and Germany and France he has a vote, but of what considerable use is it to him? He doesn't seem to know how to apply it to the best effect. With all his splendid capacities and all his fat wealth he is to-day not politically important in any country. In America, as early as 1854, the ignorant Irish hod-carrier, who had a spirit of his own and a way of exposing it to the weather, made it apparent to all that he must be politically reckoned with; yet fifteen years before that we hardly knew what an Irishman looked like.

As an intelligent force and numerically, he has always been away down, but he has governed the country just the same. It was because he was organized. It made his vote valuable — in fact, essential.

You will say the Jew is everywhere numerically feeble. That is nothing to the point—with the Irishman's history for an object-lesson. But I am coming to your numerical feebleness presently. In all parliamentary countries you could no doubt elect Jews to the legislatures—and even one member in such a body is sometimes a force which counts. How deeply have you concerned yourselves about this in Austria, France, and Germany? Or even in America, for that matter? You remark that the Jews were not to blame for the riots in this Reichsrath here, and you add with satisfaction that there wasn't one in that body. That is not strictly correct; if it were, would it not be in order for you to explain it and apologize for it, not try to make a merit of it?

But I think that the Jew was by no means in as large force there as he ought to have been, with his chances. Austria opens the suffrage to him on fairly liberal terms, and it must surely be his own fault that he is so much in the background politically. As to your numerical weakness. I mentioned some figures awhile ago—500,000—as the Jewish population of Germany. I will add some more—6,000,000 in Russia, 5,000,000 in Austria, 250,000 in the United States. I take them from memory; I read them in the Cyclopaedia Britannica ten or twelve years ago. Still, I am entirely sure of them.

If those statistics are correct, my argument is not as strong as it ought to be as concerns America, but it still has strength. It is plenty strong enough as concerns Austria, for ten years ago 5,000,000 was nine per cent. of the empire's population. The Irish would govern the Kingdom of Heaven if they had a strength there like that.

I have some suspicions; I got them at second-hand, but they have remained with me these ten or twelve years. When I read in the C. B. that the Jewish population of the United States was 250,000, I wrote the editor, and explained to him that I was personally acquainted with more Jews than that in my country, and that his figures were without a doubt a misprint for 25,000,000. I also added that I was personally acquainted with that many there; but that was only to raise his confidence in me, for it was not true.

His answer miscarried, and I never got it; but I went around talking about the matter, and people told me they had reason to suspect that for business reasons many Jews whose dealings were mainly with the Christians did not report themselves as Jews in the census. It looked plausible; it looks plausible yet. Look at the city of New York; and look at Boston, and Philadelphia, and New Orleans, and Chicago, and Cincinnati, and San Francisco—how your race swarms in those places!—and everywhere else in America, down to the least little village.

Read the signs on the marts of commerce and on the shops; Goldstein (gold stone), Edelstein (precious stone), Blumenthal (flower-vale), Rosenthal (rose-vale), Veilchenduft (violet odor), Singvogel (song-bird), Rosenzweig (rose branch), and all the amazing list of beautiful and enviable names which Prussia and Austria glorified you with so long ago. It is another instance of Europe's coarse and cruel persecution of your race; not that it was coarse and cruel to outfit it with pretty and poetical names like those, but that it was coarse and cruel to make it pay for them or else take such hideous and often indecent names that to-day their owners never use them; or, if they do, only on official papers.

And it was the many, not the few, who got the odious names, they being too poor to bribe the officials to grant them better ones. Now why was the race renamed? I have been told that in Prussia it was given to using fictitious names, and often changing them, so as to beat the tax-gatherer, escape military service, and so on; and that finally the idea was hit upon of furnishing all the inmates of a house with one and the same surname, and then holding the house responsible right along for those inmates, and accountable for any disappearances that might occur; it made the Jews keep track of each other, for self-interest's sake, and saved the government the trouble.[3]

If that explanation of how the Jews of Prussia came to be renamed is correct, if it is true that they fictitiously registered themselves to gain certain advantages, it may possibly be true that in America they refrain from registering themselves as Jews to fend off the damaging prejudices of the Christian customer. I have no way of knowing whether this notion is well founded or not. There may be other and better ways of explaining why only that poor little 250,000 of our Jews got into the Cyclopaedia. I may, of course, be mistaken, but I am strongly of the opinion that we have an immense Jewish population in America.

Point No. 3.

"Can Jews do anything to improve the situation?"

I think so. If I may make a suggestion without seeming to be trying to teach my grandmother how to suck eggs, I will offer it. In our days we have learned the value of combination. We apply it everywhere—in railway systems, in trusts, in trade unions, in Salvation Armies, in minor politics, in major politics, in European Concerts. Whatever our strength may be, big or little, we organize it. We have found out that that is the only way to get the most out of it that is in it. We know the weakness of individual sticks, and the strength of the concentrated fagot.

Suppose you try a scheme like this, for instance. In England and America put every Jew on the census-book as a Jew (in case you have not been doing that). Get up volunteer regiments composed of Jews solely, and, when the drum beats, fall in and go to the front, so as to remove the reproach that you have few Massenas among you, and that you feed on a country but don't like to fight for it. Next, in politics, organize you strength, band together, and deliver the casting vote where you can, and, where you can't, compel as good terms as possible.

You huddle to yourselves already in all countries, but you huddle to no sufficient purpose, politically speaking. You do not seem to be organized, except for your charities. There you are omnipotent; there you compel your due of recognition—you do not have to beg for it. It shows what you can do when you band together for a definite purpose. And then from America and England you can encourage your race in Austria, France, and Germany, and materially help it.

It was a pathetic tale that was told by a poor Jew in Galicia a fortnight ago during the riots, after he had been raided by the Christian peasantry and despoiled of everything he had. He said his vote was of no value to him, and he wished he could be excused from casting it, for, indeed, casting it was a sure damage to him, since no matter which party he voted for, the other party would come straight and take its revenge out of him.

Nine per cent. of the population of the empire, these Jews, and apparently they cannot put a plank into any candidate's platform! If you will send our Irish lads over here I think they will organize your race and change the aspect of the Reichsrath.

You seem to think that the Jews take no hand in politics here, that they are "absolutely non-participants." I am assured by men competent to speak that this is a very large error, that the Jews are exceedingly active in politics all over the empire, but that they scatter their work and their votes among the numerous parties, and thus lose the advantages to be had by concentration. I think that in America they scatter too, but you know more about that than I do.

Speaking of concentration, Dr. Herzl has a clear insight into the value of that. Have you heard of his plan? He wishes to gather the Jews of the world together in Palestine, with a government of their own—under the suzerainty of the Sultan, I suppose. At the Convention of Berne, last year, there were delegates from everywhere, and the proposal was received with decided favor.

I am not the Sultan, and I am not objecting; but if that concentration of the cunningest brains in the world were going to be made in a free country (bar Scotland), I think it would be politic to stop it. It will not be well to let the race find out its strength. If the horses knew theirs, we should not ride any more.

Point No. 5.

"Will the persecution of the Jews ever come to an end?"

On the score of religion, I think it has already come to an end. On the score of race prejudice and trade, I have the idea that it will continue. That is, here and there in spots about the world, where a barbarous ignorance and a sort of mere animal civilization prevail; but I do not think that elsewhere the Jew need now stand in any fear of being robbed and raided.

Among the high civilizations he seems to be very comfortably situated indeed, and to have more than his proportionate share of the prosperities going. It has that look in Vienna. I suppose the race prejudice cannot be removed; but he can stand that; it is no particular matter. By his make and ways he is substantially a foreigner wherever he may be, and even the angels dislike a foreigner. I am using this word foreigner in the German sense—stranger. Nearly all of us have an antipathy to a stranger, even of our own nationality. We pile gripsacks in a vacant seat to keep him from getting it; and a dog goes further, and does as a savage would—challenges him on the spot.

The German dictionary seems to make no distinction between a stranger and a foreigner; in its view a stranger is a foreigner—a sound position, I think. You will always be by ways and habits and predilections substantially strangers—foreigners—wherever you are, and that will probably keep the race prejudice against you alive. But you were the favorites of Heaven originally, and your manifold and unfair prosperities convince me that you have crowded back into that snug place again.

Here is an incident that is significant. Last week in Vienna a hailstorm struck the prodigious Central Cemetery and made wasteful destruction there. In the Christian part of it, according to the official figures, 621 window-panes were broken; more than 900 singing-birds were killed; five great trees and many small ones were torn to shreds and the shreds scattered far and wide by the wind; the ornamental plants and other decorations of the graves were ruined, and more than a hundred tomb-lanterns shattered; and it took the cemetery's whole force of 300 laborers more than three days to clear away the storm's wreckage. In the report occurs this remark — and in its italics you can hear it grit its Christian teeth ". . . lediglich die israelitische Abtheilung des Friedhofes vom Hagelwetter ganzlich verschont worden war." Not a hailstone hit the Jewish reservation! Such nepotism makes me tired.

Point No. 6.

"What has become of the Golden Rule?"

It exists, it continues to sparkle, and is well taken care of. It is Exhibit A in the Church's assets, and we pull it out every Sunday and give it an airing. But you are not permitted to try to smuggle it into this discussion, where it is irrelevant and would not feel at home. It is strictly religious furniture, like an acolyte, or a contribution-plate, or any of those things. It has never been intruded into business; and Jewish persecution is not a religious passion, it is a business passion.

To conclude. — If the statistics are right, the Jews constitute but one per cent. of the human race. It suggests a nebulous dim puff of star-dust lost in the blaze of the Milky Way. Properly the Jew ought hardly to be heard of; but he is heard of, has always been heard of. He is as prominent on the planet as any other people, and his commercial importance is extravagantly out of proportion to the smallness of his bulk. His contributions to the world's list of great names in literature, science, art, music, finance, medicine, and abstruse learning are also away out of proportion to the weakness of his numbers.

He has made a marvellous fight in this world, in all the ages; and has done it with his hands tied behind him. He could be vain of himself, and be excused for it. The Egyptian, the Babylonian, and the Persian rose, filled the planet with sound and splendor, then faded to dream-stuff and passed away; the Greek and the Roman followed, and made a vast noise, and they are gone; other peoples have sprung up and held their torch high for a time, but it burned out, and they sit in twilight now, or have vanished.

The Jew saw them all, beat them all, and is now what he always was, exhibiting no decadence, no infirmities of age, no weakening of his parts, no slowing of his energies, no dulling of his alert and aggressive mind. All things are mortal but the Jew; all other forces pass, but he remains. What is the secret of his immortality?

Postscript: The Jew As Soldier

When I published the above article in Harper's Monthly, I was ignorant - like the rest of the Christian world - of the fact that the Jew had a record as a soldier. I have since seen the official statistics, and I find that he furnished soldiers and high officers to the Revolution, the War of 1812, and the Mexican War. In the Civil War he was represented in the armies and navies of both the North and the South by 10 per cent. of his numerical strength - the same percentage that was furnished by the Christian populations of the two sections. This large fact means more than it seems to mean; for it means that the Jew's patriotism was not merely level with the Christian's, but overpassed it. When the Christian volunteer arrived in camp he got a welcome and applause, but as a rule the Jew got a snub. His company was not desired, and he was made to feel it. That he nevertheless conquered his wounded pride and sacrificed both that and his blood for his flag raises the average and quality of his patriotism above the Christian's. His record for capacity, for fidelity, and for gallant soldiership in the field is as good as any one's. This is true of the Jewish private soldiers and the Jewish generals alike. Major-General O. O. Howard speaks of one of his Jewish staff-officers as being "of the bravest and best"; of another - killed at Chancellorsville - as being "a true friend and a brave officer"; he highly praises two of his Jewish brigadier-generals; finally, he uses these strong words: "Intrinsically there are no more patriotic men to be found in the country than those who claim to be of Hebrew descent, and who served with me in parallel commands or more directly under my instructions."

Fourteen Jewish Confederate and Union families contributed, between them, fifty-one soldiers to the war. Among these, a father and three sons; and another, a father and four sons.

In the above article I was not able to endorse the common reproach that the Jew is willing to feed upon a country but not to fight for it, because I did not know whether it was true or false. I supposed it to be true, but it is not allowable to endorse wandering maxims upon supposition - except when one is trying to make out a case. That slur upon the Jew cannot hold up its head in presence of the figures of the War Department. It has done its work, and done it long and faithfully, and with high approval: it ought to be pensioned off now, and retired from active service.

Notes

↑ Here is another piece of picturesque history; and it reminds us that shabbiness and dishonesty are not the monopoly of any race or creed, but are merely human:

"Congress has passed a bill to pay $379.56 to Moses Pendergrass, of Libertyville, Missouri. The story of the reason of this liberality is pathetically interesting, and shows the sort of pickle that an honest man may get into who undertakes to do an honest job of work for Uncle Sam. In 1886 Moses Pendergrass put in a bid for the contract to carry the mail on the route from Knob Lick to Libertyville and Coffman, thirty miles a day, from July 1, 1887, for one year. He got the postmaster at Knob Lick to write the letter for him, and while Moses intended that his bid should be $400, his scribe carelessly made it $4. Moses got the contract, and did not find out about the mistake until the end of the first quarter, when he got his first pay. When he found at what rate he was working he was sorely cast down, and opened communication with the Post-Office Department.

The department informed him that he must either carry out his contract or throw it up, and that if he threw it up his bondsmen would have to pay the government $1459.85 damages. So Moses carried out his contract, walked thirty miles every week-day for a year, and carried the mail, and received for his labor $4 — or, to be accurate, $6.84; for, the route being extended after his bid was accepted, the pay was proportionately increased. Now, after ten years, a bill was finally passed to pay to Moses the difference between what he earned in that unlucky year and what he received."

The Sun, which tells the above story, says that bills were introduced in three or four Congresses for Moses' relief, and that committees repeatedly investigated his claim. It took six Congresses, containing in their persons the compressed virtues of 70,000,000 of people, and cautiously and carefully giving expression to those virtues in the fear of God and the next election, eleven years to find out some way to cheat a fellow-Christian out of about $13 on his honestly executed contract, and out of nearly $300 due him on its enlarged terms. And they succeeded.

During the same time they paid out $1,000,000,000 in pensions — a third of it unearned and undeserved. This indicates a splendid all-around competency in theft, for it starts with farthings, and works its industries all the way up to ship-loads. It may be possible that the Jews can beat this, but the man that bets on it is taking chances.

↑ The article was written in the summer of 1898. — Ed.

↑ In Austria the renaming was merely done because the Jews in some newly acquired regions had no surnames, but were mostly named Abraham and Moses, and therefore the tax-gatherer could not tell t'other from which, and was likely to lose his reason over the matter. The renaming was put into the hands of the War Department, and a charming mess the graceless young lieutenants made of it. To them a Jew was of no sort of consequence, and they labelled the race in a way to make the angels weep. As an example, take these two: Abraham Bellyache and Schmul Godbedamned. — Culled from "Namens Studien," by Karl Emil Franzos.

THE END

Taming the Bicycle

Mark Twain

In the early eighties Mark Twain learned to ride one of the old high-wheel bicycles of that period. He wrote an account of his experience, but did not offer it for publication. The form of bicycle he rode long ago became antiquated, but in the humor of his pleasantry is a quality which does not grow old.

A. B. P.

I

I thought the matter over, and concluded I could do it. So I went down a bought a barrel of Pond's Extract and a bicycle. The Expert came home with me to instruct me. We chose the back yard, for the sake of privacy, and went to work.

Mine was not a full-grown bicycle, but only a colt--a fifty-inch, with the pedals shortened up to forty-eight--and skittish, like any other colt. The Expert explained the thing's points briefly, then he got on its back and rode around a little, to show me how easy it was to do. He said that the dismounting was perhaps the hardest thing to learn, and so we would leave that to the last. But he was in error there. He found, to his surprise and joy, that all that he needed to do was to get me on to the machine and stand out of the way; I could get off, myself. Although I was wholly inexperienced, I dismounted in the best time on record. He was on that side, shoving up the machine; we all came down with a crash, he at the bottom, I next, and the machine on top.

We examined the machine, but it was not in the least injured. This was hardly believable. Yet the Expert assured me that it was true; in fact, the examination proved it. I was partly to realize, then, how admirably these things are constructed. We applied some Pond's Extract, and resumed. The Expert got on the OTHER side to shove up this time, but I dismounted on that side; so the result was as before.

The machine was not hurt. We oiled ourselves again, and resumed. This time the Expert took up a sheltered position behind, but somehow or other we landed on him again.

He was full of admiration; said it was abnormal. She was all right, not a scratch on her, not a timber started anywhere. I said it was wonderful, while we were greasing up, but he said that when I came to know these steel spider-webs I would realize that nothing but dynamite could cripple them. Then he limped out to position, and we resumed once more. This time the Expert took up the position of short-stop, and got a man to shove up behind. We got up a handsome speed, and presently traversed a brick, and I went out over the top of the tiller and landed, head down, on the instructor's back, and saw the machine fluttering in the air between me and the sun. It was well it came down on us, for that broke the fall, and it was not injured.

Five days later I got out and was carried down to the hospital, and found the Expert doing pretty fairly. In a few more days I was quite sound. I attribute this to my prudence in always dismounting on something soft. Some recommend a feather bed, but I think an Expert is better.

The Expert got out at last, brought four assistants with him. It was a good idea. These four held the graceful cobweb upright while I climbed into the saddle; then they formed in column and marched on either side of me while the Expert pushed behind; all hands assisted at the dismount.

The bicycle had what is called the "wabbles," and had them very badly. In order to keep my position, a good many things were required of me, and in every instance the thing required was against nature. That is to say, that whatever the needed thing might be, my nature, habit, and breeding moved me to attempt it in one way, while some immutable and unsuspected law of physics required that it be done in just the other way. I perceived by this how radically and grotesquely wrong had been the life-long education of my body and members. They were steeped in ignorance; they knew nothing--nothing which it could profit them to know. For instance, if I found myself falling to the right, I put the tiller hard down the other way, by a quite natural impulse, and so violated a law, and kept on going down. The law required the opposite thing--the big wheel must be turned in the direction in which you are falling. It is hard to believe this, when you are told it. And not merely hard to believe it, but impossible; it is opposed to all your notions. And it is just as hard to do it, after you do come to believe it. Believing it, and knowing by the most convincing proof that it is true, does not help it: you can't any more DO it than you could before; you can neither force nor persuade yourself to do it at first. The intellect has to come to the front, now. It has to teach the limbs to discard their old education and adopt the new.

The steps of one's progress are distinctly marked. At the end of each lesson he knows he has acquired something, and he also knows what that something is, and likewise that it will stay with him. It is not like studying German, where you mull along, in a groping, uncertain way, for thirty years; and at last, just as you think you've got it, they spring the subjunctive on you, and there you are. No--and I see now, plainly enough, that the great pity about the German language is, that you can't fall off it and hurt yourself. There is nothing like that feature to make you attend strictly to business. But I also see, by what I have learned of bicycling, that the right and only sure way to learn German is by the bicycling method. That is to say, take a grip on one villainy of it at a time, leaving that one half learned.

When you have reached the point in bicycling where you can balance the machine tolerably fairly and propel it and steer it, then comes your next task--how to mount it. You do it in this way: you hop along behind it on your right foot, resting the other on the mounting-peg, and grasping the tiller with your hands. At the word, you rise on the peg, stiffen your left leg, hang your other one around in the air in a general in indefinite way, lean your stomach against the rear of the saddle, and then fall off, maybe on one side, maybe on the other; but you fall off. You get up and do it again; and once more; and then several times.

By this time you have learned to keep your balance; and also to steer without wrenching the tiller out by the roots (I say tiller because it IS a tiller; "handle-bar" is a lamely descriptive phrase). So you steer along, straight ahead, a little while, then you rise forward, with a steady strain, bringing your right leg, and then your body, into the saddle, catch your breath, fetch a violent hitch this way and then that, and down you go again.

But you have ceased to mind the going down by this time; you are getting to light on one foot or the other with considerable certainty. Six more attempts and six more falls make you perfect. You land in the saddle comfortably, next time, and stay there--that is, if you can be content to let your legs dangle, and leave the pedals alone a while; but if you grab at once for the pedals, you are gone again. You soon learn to wait a little and perfect your balance before reaching for the pedals; then the mounting-art is acquired, is complete, and a little practice will make it simple and easy to you, though spectators ought to keep off a rod or two to one side, along at first, if you have nothing against them.

And now you come to the voluntary dismount; you learned the other kind first of all. It is quite easy to tell one how to do the voluntary dismount; the words are few, the requirement simple, and apparently undifficult; let your left pedal go down till your left leg is nearly straight, turn your wheel to the left, and get off as you would from a horse. It certainly does sound exceedingly easy; but it isn't. I don't know why it isn't but it isn't. Try as you may, you don't get down as you would from a horse, you get down as you would from a house afire. You make a spectacle of yourself every time.

II

During the eight days I took a daily lesson an hour and a half. At the end of this twelve working-hours' appreticeship I was graduated--in the rough. I was pronounced competent to paddle my own bicycle without outside help. It seems incredible, this celerity of acquirement. It takes considerably longer than that to learn horseback-riding in the rough.

Now it is true that I could have learned without a teacher, but it would have been risky for me, because of my natural clumsiness. The self-taught man seldom knows anything accurately, and he does not know a tenth as much as he could have known if he had worked under teachers; and, besides, he brags, and is the means of fooling other thoughtless people into going and doing as he himself has done. There are those who imagine that the unlucky accidents of life--life's "experiences"--are in some way useful to us. I wish I could find out how. I never knew one of them to happen twice. They always change off and swap around and catch you on your inexperienced side. If personal experience can be worth anything as an education, it wouldn't seem likely that you could trip Methuselah; and yet if that old person could come back here it is more that likely that one of the first things he would do would be to take hold of one of these electric wires and tie himself all up in a knot. Now the surer thing and the wiser thing would be for him to ask somebody whether it was a good thing to take hold of. But that would not suit him; he would be one of the self-taught kind that go by experience; he would want to examine for himself. And he would find, for his instruction, that the coiled patriarch shuns the electric wire; and it would be useful to him, too, and would leave his education in quite a complete and rounded-out condition, till he should come again, some day, and go to bouncing a dynamite-can around to find out what was in it.

But we wander from the point. However, get a teacher; it saves much time and Pond's Extract.

Before taking final leave of me, my instructor inquired concerning my physical strength, and I was able to inform him that I hadn't any. He said that that was a defect which would make up-hill wheeling pretty difficult for me at first; but he also said the bicycle would soon remove it. The contrast between his muscles and mine was quite marked. He wanted to test mine, so I offered my biceps--which was my best. It almost made him smile. He said, "It is pulpy, and soft, and yielding, and rounded; it evades pressure, and glides from under the fingers; in the dark a body might think it was an oyster in a rag." Perhaps this made me look grieved, for he added, briskly: "Oh, that's all right, you needn't worry about that; in a little while you can't tell it from a petrified kidney. Just go right along with your practice; you're all right."

Then he left me, and I started out alone to seek adventures. You don't really have to seek them--that is nothing but a phrase--they come to you.

I chose a reposeful Sabbath-day sort of a back street which was about thirty yards wide between the curbstones. I knew it was not wide enough; still, I thought that by keeping strict watch and wasting no space unnecessarily I could crowd through.

Of course I had trouble mounting the machine, entirely on my own responsibility, with no encouraging moral support from the outside, no sympathetic instructor to say, "Good! now you're doing well--good again--don't hurry--there, now, you're all right--brace up, go ahead." In place of this I had some other support. This was a boy, who was perched on a gate-post munching a hunk of maple sugar.

He was full of interest and comment. The first time I failed and went down he said that if he was me he would dress up in pillows, that's what he would do. The next time I went down he advised me to go and learn to ride a tricycle first. The third time I collapsed he said he didn't believe I could stay on a horse-car. But the next time I succeeded, and got clumsily under way in a weaving, tottering, uncertain fashion, and occupying pretty much all of the street. My slow and lumbering gait filled the boy to the chin with scorn, and he sung out, "My, but don't he rip along!" Then he got down from his post and loafed along the sidewalk, still observing and occasionally commenting. Presently he dropped into my wake and followed along behind. A little girl passed by, balancing a wash-board on her head, and giggled, and seemed about to make a remark, but the boy said, rebukingly, "Let him alone, he's going to a funeral."

I have been familiar with that street for years, and had always supposed it was a dead level; but it was not, as the bicycle now informed me, to my surprise. The bicycle, in the hands of a novice, is as alert and acute as a spirit-level in the detecting the delicate and vanishing shades of difference in these matters. It notices a rise where your untrained eye would not observe that one existed; it notices any decline which water will run down. I was toiling up a slight rise, but was not aware of it. It made me tug and pant and perspire; and still, labor as I might, the machine came almost to a standstill every little while. At such times the boy would say: "That's it! take a rest--there ain't no hurry. They can't hold the funeral without YOU."

Stones were a bother to me. Even the smallest ones gave me a panic when I went over them. I could hit any kind of a stone, no matter how small, if I tried to miss it; and of course at first I couldn't help trying to do that. It is but natural. It is part of the ass that is put in us all, for some inscrutable reason.

It was at the end of my course, at last, and it was necessary for me to round to. This is not a pleasant thing, when you undertake it for the first time on your own responsibility, and neither is it likely to succeed. Your confidence oozes away, you fill steadily up with nameless apprehensions, every fiber of you is tense with a watchful strain, you start a cautious and gradual curve, but your squirmy nerves are all full of electric anxieties, so the curve is quickly demoralized into a jerky and perilous zigzag; then suddenly the nickel-clad horse takes the bit in its mouth and goes slanting for the curbstone, defying all prayers and all your powers to change its mind--your heart stands still, your breath hangs fire, your legs forget to work, straight on you go, and there are but a couple of feet between you and the curb now. And now is the desperate moment, the last chance to save yourself; of course all your instructions fly out of your head, and you whirl your wheel AWAY from the curb instead of TOWARD it, and so you go sprawling on that granite-bound inhospitable shore. That was my luck; that was my experience. I dragged myself out from under the indestructible bicycle and sat down on the curb to examine.

I started on the return trip. It was now that I saw a farmer's wagon poking along down toward me, loaded with cabbages. If I needed anything to perfect the precariousness of my steering, it was just that. The farmer was occupying the middle of the road with his wagon, leaving barely fourteen or fifteen yards of space on either side. I couldn't shout at him--a beginner can't shout; if he opens his mouth he is gone; he must keep all his attention on his business. But in this grisly emergency, the boy came to the rescue, and for once I had to be grateful to him. He kept a sharp lookout on the swiftly varying impulses and inspirations of my bicycle, and shouted to the man accordingly:

"To the left! Turn to the left, or this jackass 'll run over you!" The man started to do it. "No, to the right, to the right! Hold on! THAT won't do!--to the left!--to the right!--to the LEFT--right! left--ri-- Stay where you ARE, or you're a goner!"

And just then I caught the off horse in the starboard and went down in a pile. I said, "Hang it! Couldn't you SEE I was coming?"

"Yes, I see you was coming, but I couldn't tell which WAY you was coming. Nobody could--now, COULD they? You couldn't yourself--now, COULD you? So what could _I_ do?"

There was something in that, and so I had the magnanimity to say so. I said I was no doubt as much to blame as he was.

Within the next five days I achieved so much progress that the boy couldn't keep up with me. He had to go back to his gate-post, and content himself with watching me fall at long range.

There was a row of low stepping-stones across one end of the street, a measured yard apart. Even after I got so I could steer pretty fairly I was so afraid of those stones that I always hit them. They gave me the worst falls I ever got in that street, except those which I got from dogs. I have seen it stated that no expert is quick enough to run over a dog; that a dog is always able to skip out of his way. I think that that may be true: but I think that the reason he couldn't run over the dog was because he was trying to. I did not try to run over any dog. But I ran over every dog that came along. I think it makes a great deal of difference. If you try to run over the dog he knows how to calculate, but if you are trying to miss him he does not know how to calculate, and is liable to jump the wrong way every time. It was always so in my experience. Even when I could not hit a wagon I could hit a dog that came to see me practice. They all liked to see me practice, and they all came, for there was very little going on in our neighborhood to entertain a dog. It took time to learn to miss a dog, but I achieved even that.

I can steer as well as I want to, now, and I will catch that boy one of these days and run over HIM if he doesn't reform.

Get a bicycle. You will not regret it, if you live.

THE END

Printed in the USA
CPSIA information can be obtained
at www.ICGtesting.com
LVHW052249120923
758043LV00028B/564

9 781540 529800